PRAISE FOR *THE MYSTERY PLAY*

MacDonald has crafted a deliciously twisty "what-if," populated with compelling characters, spectral thrills, and bluenose ghosts.

—AMI MCKAY
New York Times bestselling author of *The Birth House* and *The Witches of New York*

The writing is bright, poetic, surprising and funny. And to top it off, *The Mystery Play* really is a mystery, as well as a ghost story and a love story.

—WENDY LILL
Award-winning author of *The Glace Bay Miners' Museum* and *Memories of You*

MacDonald's *The Mystery Play* has four vulnerable characters seeking connection, but at its core is a rollicking good story – really creepy, very mysterious, with unexpected twists to keep an audience wondering. MacDonald beautifully marries his characters' authentic hearts with an existential "mystery."

—CATHERINE BANKS
Governor General's Award–winning author of *It Is Solved by Walking* and *Bone Cage*

MacDonald deftly blends East Coast shipbuilding and seagoing history with contemporary skepticism to come up with a drama that briskly questions the very meaning of mystery itself.

—*VIEW 902* (Halifax)

A creepy vibe … fun surprises … Sister Salter is back on the case.

—*THE COAST* (Halifax)

THE MYSTERY PLAY

ALSO BY JOSH MACDONALD

Degrees
*Halo**
*Whereverville**

*Published by Talonbooks

THE MYSTERY PLAY

A SISTER SALTER MYSTERY

a play by

Josh MacDonald

Talonbooks

Talonbooks

278 East First Avenue, Vancouver, British Columbia, Canada V5T 1A6
talonbooks.com

First printing: 2018

Typeset in Baskerville
Printed and bound in Canada on 100% post-consumer recycled paper

Cover design by Typesmith
Interior design by andrea bennett

Talonbooks acknowledges the financial support of the Canada Council
for the Arts, the Government of Canada through the Canada Book
Fund, and the Province of British Columbia through the British
Columbia Arts Council and the Book Publishing Tax Credit.

Rights to produce *The Mystery Play*, in whole or in part, in any medium
by any group, amateur or professional, are retained by the author.
Interested persons are requested to contact Kensington Literary
Representation, 34 St. Andrew Street, Toronto, Ontario, M5T 1K6;
TELEPHONE: 416-848-9648; EMAIL: kensingtonlit@rogers.com.

LIBRARY AND ARCHIVES CANADA CATALOGUING IN PUBLICATION

MacDonald, Josh, 1971–, author

    The mystery play / a play by Josh MacDonald.

ISBN 978-1-77201-216-3 (SOFTCOVER)

    I. Title.

PS8575.D642M97 2018   C812'.6   C2018-903595-1

For Conrad Byers

Fare well, seafarer.

CONTENTS

PRODUCTION HISTORY

The Mystery Play was first produced by Ship's Company Theatre in Parrsboro, Nova Scotia. It opened on August 9, 2017, with the following cast and crew:

Sister Vivian "Viv" SALTER	Mary-Colin Chisholm
GEORGE Salter	Don Allison
PETER Craig	Henricus Gielis
JENNIFER Craig	Micha Cromwell

Director: Natasha MacLellan
Set Designer: Sean Mulcahy
Lighting Designer: Leigh Ann Vardy
Costume Designer: Andrea Ritchie
Sound Designer: Joe Micallef
Technical Director: Justin Dakai
Head Carpenter: Jonah Lerner
Carpenter: Jess Preece
Technician: Trent Logan
Stage Manager: Ingrid Risk
Apprentice Stage Manager: Carmen Lee

This script was written with the financial assistance of Arts Nova Scotia, and developed at the Playwrights Atlantic Resource Centre's 2017 PARC Playwrights' Colony.

SETTING

The downstairs floor of an old house, and its adjoining in-law suite,
on Whitehall Road in Parrsboro, Nova Scotia, Canada.

CHARACTERS

Sister Vivian "Viv" SALTER, in her fifties
GEORGE Salter, in his seventies
PETER Craig, in his twenties
JENNIFER Craig, in her twenties

PLAYWRIGHT'S NOTE

Sister Vivian Salter was already in Parrsboro, Nova Scotia, before I got there.

Viv's character was established in a first play, written by Joanne Miller, starring Mary-Colin Chisholm, and produced by Ship's Company Theatre in 2015. In that first show, our Catholic nun with the sharp mind-and-tongue returned to Parrsboro in order to take care of her ailing father, while also getting embroiled in a municipal murder mystery.

I wanted this second play to keep Sister Vivian at home, with story events that perhaps *hit* her a bit closer to home. I wanted Sister Viv to question some things about herself: How can she be a rationalist and a crime solver, insistent upon proof, while *also* believing in a faith that, by definition, can't be empirically proved?

I wanted Viv to question her entire relationship to "mystery" – from the "Mysteries of the Rosary," as she'd call them, to the "Mysteries of Faith" that extend beyond our natural world, and imply the supernatural.

If I could, I wanted this one to be both a mystery play *and* a Mystery Play.

ACT ONE

The set straddles a line between kitchen-sink realism and memory-play reverie: entrances and exits are through tangible doors and the like, but the edges of the set erode into skeletal frames. Where it counts, the set is solid: allowing for angles and shadows and hidden sightlines, as such moments prove necessary.

Dominating three quarters of the set is a functioning kitchen in the middle of renovation. Windows with blinds are upstage, as well as a door to "outside." There is another doorway at stage left, with a false staircase to "upstairs." In the kitchen are a table and a few chairs. A lamp hangs from the ceiling, above the kitchen table. The kitchen floor is covered in an opaque, plastic drop cloth. Hidden beneath that drop cloth is a trapdoor to the "basement."

During the play, the ceiling's beams will become increasingly exposed. These are smaller wooden beams and joists, as well as one thick, primary timber beam. Older and greater than the rest, this timber beam threads the length of the entire set.

Beyond the implication of a dividing wall, to stage right of the kitchen, is a smaller, separate in-law suite. This suite has a curtained upstage window, and then a vestibule to "outside" at upstage right. In this vestibule are a door out (stage right), a very narrow door to the basement (centre stage), and another false staircase to upstairs (stage left).

The "renos" are taking place in the primary living area, and not in the in-law suite. The renovated decor has a younger, more metropolitan vibe, while the in-law suite looks like it hasn't changed since the late 1960s.

Currently, this entire set is dark.

In a spotlight at extreme downstage, there is an empty tailor's dummy – a "Judy" – on a pedestal.

From out of the dark, Sister Vivian SALTER steps forward. She is wearing the full, stern habit of a nun, but her traditional whites beneath the tunic present as an eerie, glow-in-the-dark green. Around her neck is a Catholic rosary, the cross and beads of which are also luminous green in the dark. She speaks to us, in direct address.

SALTER

So the story goes, at the beginning of the thirteenth century, the Virgin Mary appeared before Saint Dominic, and, from her pale, pale hands, offered him this first *rosarium*, this delicate garland of roses.

SALTER removes the rosary from her neck, working the beads between her fingers.

SALTER

Her apparition explained to Saint Dominic that every bead of the rosary was an individual prayer, and that every set of beads was called a decade. Working through these decades, mortal beings might better become lost to their contemplations: might better come to know that we will never know every aspect of God and His Plan.

One meditation of the rosary would be called Joyful, and, during Joyful Prayers, we might discover how better to "love thy

2

neighbour." One meditation would be called Sorrowful, and, while lost in these, we might deeply consider our "contempt of the world." A third meditation would be called Glorious, and there we might pray to understand the "grace of a happy death."

"And each of these meditations," said Mary's apparition, "containing all five of these decades, shall be known as the Mysteries."

> *SALTER hangs her rosary around the neck of the tailor's dummy. During her next speech, SALTER also removes the more severe aspects of her habit – her wimple, her tunic, etc. – and transfers them as well.*

SALTER

During my own last few decades, I've wondered over these Mysteries. Overmuch, I now suspect, but I'd believed them to be my mission. So how did I end up here?

> *With each item of clothes, the "Judy" looks more like a nun, and SALTER looks more everyday and civilian. At finish, SALTER wears a drab blouse and a long, unfashionable skirt.*

SALTER

After lofty, religious beginnings, my calling ... shifted. I started to wrestle with mysteries of a more pulpy and lurid kind. The kind you need a nice bottle of Purell sanitizer to wash off, when you're done.

> *SALTER rolls the dressed tailor's dummy into the in-law suite at stage right, placing it within the decor. She leaves the "Judy" there, and returns to centre stage.*

SALTER

You might wonder how a Catholic Sister even finds herself finding the drugs gone missing from a police department's evidence locker ... or how she finds herself finding the bodies that attach to the severed, and several, left feet washing onto her Haligonian harbour shores.

Well ... maybe I'm wondering how to find myself, now, too. Because I do find myself ... not quite myself; quite lost, these days, in fact.

Psalm 37:1, I believe it says, "Fret not because of evil doers," but ... the evil that men do does wear me down. Severed feet can do that to a person. The world can be rotten. And what if, perhaps, this is the only world that we ever truly get ...?

Doubts I can't help having, now that I have time to think, in my ... retreat. Waiting on my father, on our old Whitehall Road, in June. (*seeing him*) Oh, heads up, Dad –

> *Into the light, GEORGE has strayed toward SALTER. He's dishevelled, with a cardigan over an undershirt. The cardigan is misbuttoned and inside out.*

SALTER

– your buttons are all wrong.

GEORGE

What? Oh, damn, that's a dandy-o ...

> *GEORGE goes to fumble with his buttons. SALTER notices his tag is exposed.*

SALTER

You're inside out, too. Do you want me to help you?

GEORGE

I can do it.

4

She lets him. GEORGE *pulls the cardigan halfway over his head before struggling.*

GEORGE

… Heads up, I'm stuck …

SALTER

It's okay, Dad; heads up. Let's start over, maybe.

SALTER pulls her father free. Once the cardigan is removed, she begins to reset its buttons. GEORGE *stands there, adrift: vulnerable and exposed in his undershirt.* SALTER *begins to put the sweater back onto him.*

SALTER

As a young novitiate, I relished existential mysteries. In the city, I tackled criminal mysteries. But here, I spend most of my time solving the "Mystery of Dad's Missing House Keys," or the "Puzzle of Dad's Power of Attorney" … and it's these everyday things driving us both to wits' end.

With a sudden spark of anger, GEORGE *slaps* SALTER's *hand away from his buttons.*

SALTER

Ow!

GEORGE

I can do it.

SALTER

You don't have to swat me.

He does keep flailing, and he does swat her a second time.

SALTER

You don't have to swat me! (*forcibly restraining his hands*) Don't think I won't swat you back, you mean old Baptist.

GEORGE

Well, then let me be, so I can get to looking!

> *GEORGE walks upstage from SALTER, cueing lights up in the kitchen. There is an open toolbox on the counter. GEORGE yanks open kitchen drawers, then slams them again, rattling the contents within.*

SALTER

Dad always hated mysteries: he'd jump to the last page to see how they turned out. And now he's stuck in one, every day, that he can never quite solve. Because the world can be rotten.

> *SALTER follows GEORGE into this kitchen space.*

SALTER

Have you figured it out yet, Dad? What you're looking for?

GEORGE

(*still rummaging*) I can't find a goddamn thing in here.

SALTER

Because you don't live here anymore. Neither of us do.

> *This creates a moment of real confusion for GEORGE: he's stopped by it.*

GEORGE

… This is my house.

SALTER

You know the story: we live in the back now. In our own
separate place.

GEORGE

… This was my kitchen.

SALTER

You're right. It was. (*beat*) We do have memories in this room.

GEORGE

… Viv had a tooth so rotten, I thought she was going to
choke on it.

SALTER

That's right! That's good. But you know that I'm Viv, right?

GEORGE

She'd run around the kitchen table, trying to get away from me,
but it had to be yanked out.

SALTER

(*amused*) I was running because you were chasing me with a pair
of Vise-Grips. (*lifting a similar pair from the open toolbox*) I was
terrified; I was six, or five; and it was like my world had gone
crazy. But you promised you'd take me to the movies, if I let you
pull the tooth.

GEORGE

Not my kind of movie. Didn't wanna see it.

SALTER

Do you remember what it was, Dad? (*trying to jog his memory*)
We watched it at The Gem …? Down on Main Street?

GEORGE

… How did this goddamn room get so wrecked?

SALTER

Well, that happened more recently.

Beyond the left doorway is an implication of a stairway to upstairs. PETER Craig appears from there in a carpenter's belt and raised goggles, drinking a beer. He's ingratiating, but there can be forceful insinuations in his tone.

PETER

Some days he's further out to sea, huh?

SALTER

We won't make a routine of this.

PETER

Not a problem to let you in. What movie did he take you to?

PETER swaps some items between his carpenter's belt and his toolbox.

SALTER

Oh, I didn't mean to pull you into … I mean, we value our privacy, too.

PETER

What'd you take her to see, George? Was it *The Sound of Music*?

SALTER

I can assure you I have no interest in singing nuns.
Or flying ones.

GEORGE

How'd you know my name? What are you doing here?

PETER

We've been introduced a few times, George, but that's okay:
(*shaking hands*) I'm Peter Craig, and I bought this house from
your daughter, from Viv.

> *SALTER gives PETER a small look – she doesn't like being called*
> *"Viv" by anyone but her father, but she doesn't correct him yet.*
> *PETER interprets her look as something else –*

PETER

What, is that patronizing?

SALTER

Dad, you're on the waiting list for Mount Hope. We've talked
about that. But it might be twelve months, and the Craigs
wanted to buy now, so ... we recognized there might be
a compromise.

PETER

That's not the only thing your daughter recognized. She knew
what I did for a living, as soon as I stepped out of my car. What
my wife did too.

SALTER

You had dealer plates. She had chalk dust on her hands.
(*shrugging*) It's an old habit I'm trying to get out of. (*beat*) And I
recognize the pun in that.

PETER

For a person who doesn't use money, you knew how to bargain,
but ... no hard feelings, huh?

SALTER

Well, we're all here, aren't we? (*beat*) Good fences, good
neighbours; it's just ... when he hears the banging through the
wall, it brings him back over.

PETER

This place has some beautiful old bones, George. We're
knocking out that false ceiling; lifting the height of the room.
Look at the beams you had up there!

> *Their eyes go upward, as PETER claps his hand on the timber
> beam, on his tiptoes.*

GEORGE

Opening old wounds, jackass.

> *Before PETER can bristle, SALTER tries to explain –*

SALTER

He says things.

> *From the upstage door to outside, JENNIFER Craig enters. In her
> hands are a few sheets of onionskin paper, covered in charcoal
> grave rubbings. There's an azurite crystal pendant around her
> neck and a wild rose in her hair.*

JENNIFER

Sister Vivian, George, hello! I can't believe I'm missing our
first company.

PETER

They were just getting on their way.

SALTER

We're interrupting your privacy.

JENNIFER

Oh, no, please. We don't know anybody, and it's a beautiful afternoon. (*to PETER*) Hi.

PETER

Hi.

> *They kiss "hello." It goes on a moment longer than SALTER really needs it to, and then –*

JENNIFER

Did Peter even offer you anything?

PETER

No, 'cause I'm a jackass. (*beat*) I'm kidding, guys, it's okay: Jennifer would love you to stay.

GEORGE

I'm thirsty.

JENNIFER

Of course you are.

GEORGE

You best make it something sweet.

SALTER

You're being difficult, Dad.

> *JENNIFER puts her grave rubbings on the table, and opens the fridge – it's relatively empty.*

JENNIFER

Did you drink all those beers? We are shockingly unprepared. I have Brita water and one lemon. There's ice.

> *GEORGE grips the handle of another kitchen drawer.*

PETER

That drawer's stuck. We haven't budged it since we moved in –

Through a quirk of muscle memory, GEORGE is able to jostle this drawer open. From within it, he produces a package of Cherry Kool-Aid.

GEORGE

Ha!

SALTER

… Is that what you've been looking for?

JENNIFER

Well, life should have some treats, shouldn't it? And it's summer. Will you help me make it, George?

SALTER

You can see he's not great with new people. He's not great with me.

But throughout the next, GEORGE does assist JENNIFER. A pitcher and glasses are produced; Brita water and ice get added to the Kool-Aid mix. Eventually, GEORGE stirs it, while JENNIFER cuts the lemon into slices and drops them in.

SALTER

… Well, there you go.

JENNIFER

Sit for a minute, Sister. Your days must be tiring.

SALTER sits. Meanwhile, PETER inspects the stubborn drawer.

SALTER

I wasn't with him, for a lot of years. Him and the building have developed quirks.

From the drawer, PETER reveals a stockpiled motherlode of loose Kool-Aid packages. PETER quotes the Kool-Aid Man –

PETER

"Oh yeah."

SALTER leafs through the charcoal rubbings in front of her.

GEORGE

Where's your kids?

PETER

Um ...?

SALTER

Sorry again.

JENNIFER

We don't have any, George. But I do have students. Grades sixes and fives. (*pointing to the charcoal rubbings*) I thought that'd be a nice activity with them, come the fall.

SALTER

Grave rubbings?

JENNIFER

It's such a simple way to bring back the past.

SALTER

(*reading one*) "Love, Unforgotten ..." (*beat*) ... but then the name is faded; you can't even read it.

JENNIFER makes an association to GEORGE. She's simple and direct with him.

JENNIFER

Do you know what's making you forget, George? What it's called?

GEORGE

It's "All's ... Hell's ..." (*frustrated*) Tsk, that word. (*trying for "Alzheimer's"*) It's "All's Hell's Hammers"?

SALTER

Yes, Dad, you can say that again. It's All's Hell's Hammers.

JENNIFER

(*indicating that grave rubbing*) But love remains, no matter what. That's what this represents.

SALTER

I think this more clearly represents "death."

JENNIFER

Well, Sister, that's how we're different. Different auras.

PETER takes the wild rose out of JENNIFER's hair. They're a couple in the flush of love.

SALTER

We could probably enumerate more differences.

SALTER drinks from her Kool-Aid, and grimaces at the overall sweetness.

SALTER

Uck. No wonder my teeth fell out.

❖   ❖   ❖

Lighting change: spotlight at the front of the stage. SALTER comes forward, with GEORGE. She helps him remove his cardigan again, reducing him to his undershirt.

SALTER

Later that night, I catch him in conversation with no one.

GEORGE

Oh, I know, it's a crime!

SALTER

I put myself in front of him, and he doesn't see me –

GEORGE

If Viv always needs to have the last word, she won't make any friends.

SALTER

I'm fifty-eight, Dad …

He exits. She continues, to herself.

SALTER

… And you wouldn't be wrong.

SALTER addresses us directly again.

SALTER

The Craigs seemed like the perfect couple … until they didn't. I wished I could believe in their "auras," but …

At first, forgive me, Jennifer Craig was so chipper it made me want to feed her into a wood chipper. And Peter Craig was my quintessence of a used-car salesman: having convinced me, even with no down payment, that a second offer would never arrive on this house, and that he was my best deal.

The two of them presented as the story of True Love: married for only a clutch of moments, and having just met for the first time in the previous twelve months. Twelve months! It wasn't just the contents of their fridge that made them seem "shockingly unprepared."

Lighting change: half-light up on the kitchen, behind SALTER. JENNIFER places her charcoal rubbing on the door of the fridge using magnets – "Love, Unforgotten."

Next, PETER and JENNIFER perform renovation tasks, like they're in a dumb show. They affix a plastic sheet over their exposed cabinets and the counter below. The "drape" of this sheet will protect the cabinets' plates, cups, glasses, etc. from construction dust.

SALTER

But they'd leaped, like young couples do, believing that for them it would magically work out. That somehow they wouldn't fall out of love with Love; be exhausted by it, like any number of "God's given blessings" …

… Or maybe that's just me.

During the couple's dumb show activities, dusky light begins to play through the kitchen window above one counter. Eventually, the venetian blinds to this window get closed.

SALTER

From the honeymoon windows of the main house, the Craigs looked backwards by twelve months and saw nothing but their happy beginnings. Me, I looked forward by another twelve, and saw depositing my father into Mount Hope –

his mind emptied – and then what would happen to him next, no mystery.

From my perspective – having lived longer than many True Lovers – the truest kind of love is having to watch someone die.

It's only him and me. And then ... it'll only be me. And then, after that, well then ... well ...

But Mary also gave us the Joyful Mysteries, if you can make yourself believe. "Love thy neighbour."

>   *SALTER cedes the floor to the Craigs, with a tip of her hand. She exits.*

>   *Lighting change: practical lamps turn on in the kitchen, as the Craigs quit their repairs for the night. JENNIFER sits at the kitchen table, and PETER massages her neck.*

PETER

I feel like if she was a car, I'd have to disclose it, like, "Watch out: lemon, bitter."

JENNIFER

I think she's interesting!

PETER

I think she's an endangered species.

JENNIFER

(*laughing*) She did us a kindness, you know. We are here.

PETER

I know. (*beat*) I'm gonna get my credit undicked. I promise.

JENNIFER

You're going to hate that commute.

PETER

Naw ... Driving every day to Truro? What's not to love?

JENNIFER and PETER

It's the Hub!

JENNIFER

Thank you for moving here. For me.

PETER

Back in the day, it was the nuns who taught. You,
they're gonna love.

JENNIFER

... A place where we don't have to lock our door. (*beat*) Welcome
home, husband.

PETER

Welcome home, wife. (*kissing the top of her head*) I was done
with the city when they siphoned the gas out of our chained-up
lawnmower, that's when I was done.

JENNIFER laughs.

PETER

No, I could have murdered that guy.

JENNIFER

For a three-dollar offence?

PETER

I've got a lot of rage.

*He creeps his hands from a "neck massage" to a "choke
hold." She laughs more, and squirms, and gives him a shot
with her elbow –*

JENNIFER

Who are you, right now?? (*joking*) Release your chakras, man!

*They begin to wrestle, like it might become something romantic.
But they startle and freeze at a very loud banging from the
kitchen door to outside – BANG! BANG! BANG!*

PETER

Yikes! What the hell?

JENNIFER

(*beat; hushed*) It's almost midnight – who'd …?

PETER

She's not our landlady. What's she – We're not even
doing anything!

JENNIFER

Maybe something's wrong. Maybe you should get it.

Three more insistent bangs: BANG! BANG! BANG!

*Getting annoyed, PETER moves to open the door, calling to
the other side.*

PETER

Yeah! Yeah, yeah, we hear you! We're coming!

*He yanks the door open, revealing nothing but darkness. No one
is there. The couple exchange a wordless frown, and then PETER
steps beyond the door jamb to look in either direction. He steps
back inside, then closes the door.*

PETER

If it was the old guy, well, he doesn't move that fast. That was … weird.

JENNIFER

Do you know what a forerunner is?

PETER

No.

JENNIFER

I read about it, prepping the grave rubbings. It's three knocks on a door, and then … nothing there.

PETER

In folklore?

JENNIFER

Yeah. It's supposed to be like a … ghost, or like a … death is coming?

PETER

Well, good. Maybe it's the guy who siphoned our gas.

BANG! BANG! BANG! But this time, it's the more brittle sound of a fist on a window pane. JENNIFER decides that she's closest and gestures "shhh" to PETER. She silently hops backwards onto the kitchen counter, putting her back flush to the wall. She twists the wand of the blinds beside her, angling open the window's slats. Again, there's just darkness out there.

JENNIFER

I can't see anything.

JENNIFER pivots the blinds closed again. PETER makes his way to the room's lamp.

PETER

Make it dark on both sides.

> *He snaps out the lamp, changing the balance of light. Now it's very dark inside, and somewhat brighter outside, beyond those closed blinds.*

PETER

Just rip off the bandage: one, two –

PETER and JENNIFER

Three!

> *This time, JENNIFER hauls on the drawstring at the other side of the wand. The venetian blind zips up in full – revealing the backlit form of a woman in a nun's habit, her face turned upstage from the glass.*

> *JENNIFER yelps on reflex, and leaps from the kitchen counter. PETER yelps as well.*

PETER

God DAMMIT!

> *PETER rips the door open and runs outside to confront the figure. PETER's visible beyond the glass, as he slows down and becomes puzzled ...*

JENNIFER

What is it?

> *PETER swivels the figure downstage, so JENNIFER can see it through the window. It's only the tailor's dummy from the opening scene, dressed in SALTER's full regalia.*

PETER

Well. Someone put it out here.

JENNIFER moves upstage to the open door, her attention on her husband in the dark.

JENNIFER

Peter, let's deal with this tomorrow. Just come back in for tonight.

PETER picks up the tailor's "Judy" and hikes it over his shoulder. He marches past the window and the open door, toward SALTER's in-law suite.

JENNIFER's attention follows him.

JENNIFER

What do you think you're going to accomplish?

PETER

I'm gonna use it as a battering ram, if they don't answer the door.

But through these last bits of business, all aimed upstage, something has been happening centre stage. It is visible to the audience, but not to PETER and JENNIFER, in their distraction ...

... the trap door, hidden beneath the plastic drop cloth, opens, with its hinge downstage. Slowly rising from out of this trap, yet always remaining beneath the opaque drop cloth, is an emerging human figure, visible only in filmy silhouette.

A supernatural amount of light gushes upward, from inside the trap.

Upstage, JENNIFER grows to a slow-dawning awareness that this is taking place behind her. She turns ...

Disembodied from any source now, the sound of supernatural booming grows deafening, while the figure fully rises from the trap.

BOOOOM! BOOOOOM!! BOOOOOOM!!!

Almost delicately, with horror and awe, JENNIFER reaches out to the draped figure. She puts her hand to the lit-from-beneath sheet, and after a beat ... she yanks it free.

Lighting change: instant transition to a new, naturalistic, daytime scene. GEORGE stands revealed in the centre of the room, emerged from under the opaque sheet. He is slump-shouldered, facing upstage. The trap door is still open. PETER and SALTER enter. Nerves are frayed between them all; there's a noticeable difference in PETER and JENNIFER's dynamic. (Note: During this scene, at some point, JENNIFER should roll down the sleeves of her top, all the way to her wrists. Also during this scene, at some point, PETER should roll up his sleeves: revealing hip, semi-tough tattoos, with a sailor's bent.)

PETER

(*accusatory*) So what are we gonna do here, Viv? What do we do?

SALTER

Not talk at your current decibel: this doesn't help him.

PETER

Help him?? Listen, I think I've been very patient –

SALTER

Oh, a saint.

23

PETER

- while things are going through the roof over here! I'm serious!

JENNIFER

(*like a teacher*) Time out, okay? (*beat*) I agree with the both of you. The last few weeks, it is getting worse ... and I think we could talk about it, calmly.

GEORGE

... talk about me, like I'm a goddamn ghost ...

JENNIFER

I'm sorry, George. I was only talking about the situation.

SALTER

And I apologize. Of course I do. For him and me. (*weary*) I have to fall asleep at some point, and short of tying him down ...

PETER opens a kitchen drawer and removes a bicycle lock made of chain. It's almost like he's insinuating "Let's tie him up with this." But then he clarifies –

PETER

... It's for the basement.

PETER kneels at the hatch, and shuts it. Once closed, he threads the bike chain through eyelets there, locking the trap door.

PETER

We start locking our doors, and your Dad comes through the windows. We lock our windows, and he comes through the cellar. Obviously, we're not gonna involve the police –

JENNIFER

– Obviously! But what about a doctor? When's the last time you saw one?

SALTER

We have an appointment with the doctor next week,
don't we, Dad?

GEORGE

… Yeah, heads up, he can go to hell …

> *GEORGE rummages in the neighbour's kitchen cupboards.*
> *SALTER tries to curb him.*

SALTER

You can't be in their stuff, Dad.

GEORGE

(*muttering*) Old wounds, I'll fix them …

> *GEORGE swats her again.*

SALTER

He's fixated on something. He can't rest.

PETER

No one's resting, Viv.

SALTER

I've been meaning to say: nobody calls me "Viv," except my
father, so –

> *GEORGE finds a glass jar in the shape of a bear, filled to*
> *the brim with loose coins. He spills them out, loudly, across*
> *the counter.*

PETER

(*beat; nonplussed*) Did you find what you were looking for …?

> *GEORGE works his way through the coins, inspecting them,*
> *one by one …*

PETER

I lost my pair of Vise-Grips. You remember them, Sister Viv?
From a few weeks back?

JENNIFER

Peter ...

SALTER

I can look for them at our place, if that's what you're suggesting.

PETER

I just don't know where else they'd go.

SALTER

It is a symptom. Shiny things, things he gives importance, but ...
we made a Memory Box for that reason, didn't we, Dad? It's
where those objects end up. (*withering*) And I didn't see your
Vise-Grips in there.

PETER

I just don't know where else they'd go.

JENNIFER

God, Peter, give it a rest.

PETER

Do you want to fight with me, too?

JENNIFER

No. We're all in this together.

PETER

Are we, though?? (*beat*) Am I responsible for him?

GEORGE

Mind your tone, jackass!

PETER

Is that my second job, when I come back from my first job?

SALTER

Dad –

PETER

Or, I'm sorry, is that my third job when I finish your designer's showcase? (*pointing at the ceiling*)

JENNIFER

You know, I can locate one "tool" in this room right now. (*meaning him*)

> *SALTER is impressed, amused, but squashes it. PETER deflates.*

PETER

Okay. I'm officially not at my best.

GEORGE

Get out, if you can't mind your damn tone!!

JENNIFER

… You heard him.

PETER

Yeah. I am already late, so …

> *PETER exits. Soon after, the sounds of a car as it drives away.*

> *SALTER puts her hands on GEORGE and he swats her again. This time she snaps.*

SALTER

Alright, that's it!

> *It's JENNIFER who tries to defuse things, with a new tack.*

JENNIFER

George? Would you like to count these coins together?

GEORGE

… Yeah. Dandy-o.

> *GEORGE calms, with a new task at hand. JENNIFER clinks coins*
> *back into the jar.*

GEORGE

Where's your kids?

> *JENNIFER sighs, her positivity flagging ... SALTER notices.*

SALTER

I know. It frays the nerves.

JENNIFER

(*stony*) I want you to come over anytime he's not here. (*beat*)
If you need to come over, George, then, of course, you will. It'll
be a secret we have.

> *Lighting change: centre spotlight. SALTER steps forward, and the*
> *others exit.*

SALTER

This hadn't happened over a day, but over a series of days:
each gaining on the one before it, like the tidal creep toward
full moon in Parrsboro Harbour. Flooding over our heads,
it seemed, just a bit higher, every thirteen hours.

So: something new, to try to keep our heads above water.

Lighting change: evening lights up on the in-law suite, on stage right. The window here has its curtains drawn.

SALTER walks past the dividing wall, and into the in-law suite. GEORGE is seated here, stripped to his undershirt. We can see an Exelon medical patch on GEORGE's right shoulder blade. SALTER prepares another, from a prescription box.

SALTER

You have to try to remember this too, okay, Dad?

She peels away GEORGE's old patch.

GEORGE

Ow!

SALTER

Oh, that's not "ow." (*mid-task*) It's just a matter of removing the old patch, every day, before we put the new one on. Doctor's orders.

She sticks a new patch over the same spot.

SALTER

If you end up wearing both patches, well, you might get faint. It's a side effect.

She helps him shrug back into his cardigan, and re-button it.

SALTER

If it does work, though ... some things might come back to you.

GEORGE

Like Viv?

SALTER

(*frowns*) ... I'm Viv.

29

GEORGE

No. Viv left me. (*beat*) You're the old nun who visits.

SALTER

(*stung*) I know you don't mean to be mean, but sometimes ...

GEORGE

(*exiting upstairs*) ... old wounds ...

SALTER

... I wonder.

> *SALTER watches him go. She looks tired, defeated. After a beat, she resumes direct address, in the in-law suite.*
>
> *On the other side of the dividing wall, in the darkness of the Craigs' kitchen, PETER and JENNIFER continue to make progress on their renovations.*

SALTER

Like that Bay of Fundy, it felt like something was pumping into the house, filling it to dangerous levels, particularly on the other side of the wall. Every evening, instead of muffled conversation or casual laughter, I'd hear the obsessive hammering of hammers over there, or the crack of a crowbar through plaster, and I would wonder ...

> *We hear the agitating racket of construction, growing louder.*

SALTER

I'd wonder, overnight, when instead of newlywed noises, I'd hear the sudden shattering of a plate, or the sharp clatter of an overturned chair. Or worse, out of the 3 a.m. quiet: an angry masculine yell, or a feminine cry, quick-cut short.

All these sounds of frightening distress come from PETER and JENNIFER, barely visible as silhouettes in the dark. SALTER listens to them, grim.

SALTER

Mary gave us the Sorrowful Mysteries, to express our "contempt of the world."

But I had no contempt for Jennifer Craig. As the weeks drifted through July, I felt myself warming, too; to this person who was good to my father, in her daytime home, no matter what was happening to her in the dark.

Lighting change: dawn light, peeking around the curtains of the windows.

SALTER

And then, one dawn, I found this, written in the dew outside my window –

SALTER opens her curtains to reveal the word "VIV" traced there. "VIV" is written on the outside of the glass, in a trickling fingermark.

SALTER

– and felt I had cause to visit on my own.

SALTER picks up a cloth bag, containing a glass bottle, and crosses into the main kitchen with it.

Lighting change: morning light up in the Craigs' kitchen.

*JENNIFER sits at her empty kitchen table, subdued. She is
wearing heavier makeup than usual, and long sleeves and pants.
When SALTER arrives, standing at the other side of the table,
we're already mid-scene –*

SALTER

Should I perceive this as some kind of nocturnal taunt? Because
I don't really understand it.

JENNIFER

I don't understand why you think it was Peter.

SALTER

It's a theory we could test. (*lightly*) It's not outside my skill set,
lifting fingerprints with a makeup brush and a fine powder. Even
if it's an unlikely powder. Like Kool-Aid crystals.

JENNIFER remains wan, but eventually chuckles.

JENNIFER

… I'm never drinking that stuff again, unless it's Kool-Aid Shots.

SALTER

I've got a quicker delivery system than that.

*SALTER pulls a bottle of Cinzano from her bag, plunking it on
the table. She sits.*

JENNIFER

(*shocked; amused*) Sister! It's not even noon!

SALTER

Well, George is asleep, and Peter is gone, and how's your
summer been going?

JENNIFER

(*beat; considers*) This place is lovely, but it can be … lonely.

SALTER

I hear you, sister.

She cracks the bottle's seal.

JENNIFER

Oh, what the hell. (*grabbing two glasses*) I still have lemons and ice.

SALTER

I had to sneak this bottle over. George is a Baptist, he wouldn't approve.

JENNIFER

Your Dad's a Baptist …? (*puzzled*) But you're a … How …?

SALTER

It's a story for another day.

They make drinks. Again, JENNIFER uses a knife to cut up the fruit.

JENNIFER

Did you always know? That you had a calling?

SALTER

"Calling" presumes that you're being called to something, but I fear I was mostly running from.

JENNIFER

I never wanted to do anything but teach. (*tentative*) And you're a … sleuth … too … sometimes?

SALTER

I'm not anything right now, but Dad's. (*beat; gentle*) Oh, sometimes, I do wonder over mystery, it's true. Like ... I wonder about your long, buttoned sleeves in July, or about that makeup over your black eye.

> *Surprised, JENNIFER's hand flutters to her face. On her upstage side, she does indeed have a black eye, covered in heavy foundation.*

JENNIFER

Oh! I just ... No. I fell down. It's nothing ...

> *They each wait on the other, waiting for more information.*

SALTER

(*earnest; slowly*) Are you alright ...?

JENNIFER

It's not what you think.

SALTER

What do you think I think ...?

JENNIFER

I thought you valued your privacy.

> *SALTER considers a moment. Then she offers of herself, hoping to win JENNIFER's trust.*

SALTER

I fell in love here, a long time ago, and then I left here, in several kinds of shame. I joined the sisterhood. Dad was not pleased: we didn't recognize one another for ... quite some time.
He wished for grandchildren; instead he got "nun." (*"nun/none"* – *her glum pun.*)

SALTER takes a drink. A moment later, JENNIFER also drinks.

SALTER

So who am I to counsel about marriage? But I do know what
loneliness is. And if you need to talk, I want to be your ...

JENNIFER

What?

SALTER

... I want to be your friend.

JENNIFER

I'd like that, too. (*considering, then*) It's not about whether I love
him, or he loves me – (*grasping*) I mean, this ceiling: he's only
doing it because I wanted it; I ...

SALTER

(*about the beam above her head*) He's making progress.

JENNIFER

Now I don't even care ... (*beat*) I know he loves me, but I'm not
sure I know him; not here.

SALTER

You feel he's changed?

JENNIFER

His aura's darkening. I know you don't believe in that, but ...
He's exhausted. I'm worried he's going to fly off that road, every
day, back and forth to Truro. He hasn't been able to sell a single
car. I thought, at first, that was what was keeping him up nights.
(*beat*) What do dreams of drowning mean?

SALTER

In analysis, they might say it's a dream of being overwhelmed.
New job, new marriage, new house, tackling your own
construction ... that's a lot.

JENNIFER

I'm sleeping next to somebody I don't really know. I didn't know
he couldn't swim, until we moved here. Now he drowns in his
sleep, and he's soaked in his own sweat, and what wakes him up
is his own most horrifying gasp – like he's pulling in breath on a
punctured lung. But ... even worse is when he stays asleep, and
he walks around. (*beat*) He does things. (*grasping*) Maybe that's
when he wrote your name on the window?

SALTER

Maybe.

JENNIFER

The other night, he was drowning himself in the kitchen sink,
the water spilling past his shoulders. He was so tormented. I had
to wake him. And then it got worse still.

SALTER

How? How did you get your black eye, Jennifer?

JENNIFER

Um, I told you. I fell down. I don't know what possessed me:
I just got dizzy and I fell. I hit my head on the side of the table.

SALTER

(*with gravity*) I have known women who have told me it was
their fault, because they were clumsy. Who have hidden terrible
bruises under their sleeves. And, together, we have been able to
make sure it never happens again.

JENNIFER

Oh, no. Peter would never do that. He ... loves me.

SALTER

You've said. (*beat*) But you're still afraid.

JENNIFER has another drink.

JENNIFER

Has anything unexplainable ever happen in this house?

SALTER

Not that I know of.

JENNIFER

(*nodding, then*) When Peter woke out of the sink, he was wet,
of course. I went to get a tea towel for him, and everything
just ... shifted. Like, the atmosphere shifted? And then every
object in the room – every dish on the shelf – just pushed itself to
the right, like this:

> *JENNIFER uses her fingers to "drive" the Cinzano bottle to the
> very edge of the table. She does this deliberately, without hurry,
> by way of illustration.*

SALTER

By several inches?

JENNIFER

Yes. Things fell, things broke, I shouted. But when everything
moved right, I moved left; like my inner ear had tilted, too.
I tried to catch my feet beneath me, and then everything
shifted back ...

> *With her fingers, JENNIFER "drives" the Cinzano bottle
> back to centre.*

JENNIFER

... and that's when I fell. I hit the table pretty hard. (*beat*) But Peter was nowhere near me; he was across the room. (*beat*) Do you believe in the supernatural, Sister Vivian ...?

SALTER

(*considers, then*) While in novitiate, I learned about an entire convent of nuns said to be possessed by supernatural devils. This was in the 1700s. A French priest threw a bouquet of roses to one nun, over the convent wall. Somehow this invited the devils Asmodeus and Zabulon – devils A to Z – to lodge their way into these women's hearts. Objects flew, bodies contorted, and the righteous spoke in tongues; nuns stripped themselves of their habits, and made mountains of their flesh. And the church said these possessions were very true: so much so, that thousands of people travelled to the convent, to see the exorcisms take place.

JENNIFER

But what do you think happened?

SALTER

I think the priest was supposed to be very handsome ... and that the nuns were very repressed ... and that superhuman events often mask very human stories. I do believe it all started with a gesture of roses, though – lots of stories do – and that what perverted over time probably started as a form of True Love.

JENNIFER

... Please. I'm not telling you any kind of story, except the one that happened to me. I know how I sound, I really do, and I understand you don't believe in devils A to Z, but ...

SALTER

But what?

JENNIFER

... Don't you need to believe in ghosts, still? Holy or otherwise? (*beat*) I just ... I need help.

Lighting change: centre spotlight. SALTER steps forward.
JENNIFER clears the table and exits. An extended transition to
nighttime lighting on both playable areas of the set.

SALTER

Abusive husband or supernatural magic? (*shrugging*) Occam's razor. (*beat*) But, long ago, I had made a headstrong promise to believe in the Mysteries of Faith. So ... if we accept that aspects of God are fundamentally unknowable ... and that God exists in all things ... then shouldn't "all things" also be imbued with a piece of that unknowability? Shouldn't incredible things, supernatural things ... at least be possible?

Well ... she did need my help.

Perhaps I could start with the tangible, and do some digging. Consider the solid, archival facts ...

As SALTER speaks, she enters the playing area of the in-law
suite. It's dark here, but the word "VIV" remains visible on the
moonlit window.

SALTER

If Jennifer Craig believed the house to be haunted, had any of its previous owners believed the same? Well, George Salter, my father, had lived here for some forty-odd stubborn years, and – even with the visiting kids on Halloween nights – he wouldn't have said so. Before George Salter, the house was owned by Archie Morris, and Johnson Morris before that, with nary a bump in the night.

While SALTER's speech continues, PETER appears on the stairs near his own dark kitchen. He's in a housecoat, and his movements are the ungainly movements of a sleepwalker. He removes his claw hammer from his toolbox, and he kneels at the trapdoor. He opens the locked chain, lifts the trapdoor, and then descends out of sight, step by slow step ...

SALTER

In the records I found, there was no reason this house should be haunted. No children broke their necks, no wasting diseases, no shotgun blasts to spray a lingering grudge into the walls. In fact, the only people to die under this roof were plump and happy, in their beds, content in the knowledge that another generation was born to remember them.

Built by the Morrises in 1916, humble in comparison to other homes above the beach, the Whitehall House had a pretty clean slate.

SALTER shuts the curtains across the "VIV" window. Readying for bed, she climbs upstairs ...

SALTER

Later, in the pin-drop silence:

SALTER exits upstairs. Almost immediately, a very narrow doorway opens ...

PETER trespasses into the in-law suite, using this narrow door to enter up from the basement. If timed correctly, his exit via the trap door and his re-entrance here should feel like an unbroken, metronomic walk ...

PETER still carries the claw hammer at his side ... but everything else about him has changed. Between his descent and his ascent,

PETER is now dressed in turn-of-the-nineteenth-century clothes, and he is soaked to the bone.

PETER sloshes across the in-law suite with slow, shambling steps. His breathing is heavy.

From offstage, SALTER calls –

SALTER

Dad, are you downstairs already …?

She comes partway back down the steps –

SALTER

You need to try to sleep through the night –

She betrays a small gasp, seeing PETER in the middle of the room. For his part, PETER pivots toward the sound of her voice. His heavy breathing continues.

SALTER

Peter …?

Fascinated, cautious, SALTER comes to the bottom of the stairs. In a calming tone –

SALTER

Peter, you're not in your own home …

She casts a wide berth around the sleeping man, clocking the basement door from which he came.

SALTER

Peter, you should return to your own home.

PETER continues to pivot toward her voice, following her circumference. Slowly, he raises the hammer from his hip

to his chest level. The hammer's claw is aimed at SALTER,
intimidating. It shines in the dark.

Sound cue: Beginning softly and building to a crescendo by the
end of this sequence, the disembodied booming sound returns.

SALTER

For all my experiences, I'd never had somebody break into my
own home. It left me fumbling and unready, like the girl I was,
when I'd lived here long ago. Like the girl I was, who ran away
and never came back, as my father tells me, through his All's
Hell's Hammers ...

SALTER is being backed into the upstage left corner, near the
vestibule. PETER gains on her, leaving a trail of wet footsteps.
He raises the claw hammer high above his head, aiming it
toward SALTER.

PETER

(barely a whisper) ... Torment ...

Growing sound cue:

BOOM ...!   BOOM ...!   BOOM ...!

SALTER

And from my awful vantage, I had a moment of trying to
remember, ridiculous, whether it might be more dangerous
to wake somebody from their night terrors, or to just
leave them be ...

PETER is just upstage of SALTER now, on the other side of the
vestibule doorway.

SALTER

... while Peter raised the claw of his All's Hell's
Hammers high ...

Growing sound cue:

BOOM ...!   *BOOM ...!*   *BOOM ...!*

SALTER

... and he swung it toward me ...

> *SALTER tenses, but PETER lodges the claw hammer into the wall above her head.*

SALTER

... and above me.

> *To the tempo of the supernatural booms, PETER repeatedly dislodges and swings his hammer. He's ripping into the wall, just above the vestibule door jamb.*

> *SALTER, no longer in danger, steps free from the wall to consider PETER's obsessive action.*

SALTER

(*also in tempo*) Toward me ... and above me. Toward me ... and above me. Chewing into the pineapple-patterned wallpaper that had hung here forever, and then into the plaster beyond that, exposing the timber beneath.

> *Dust and debris fall from the excavation point, revealing the end of the beam. SALTER notices something on the beam's upstage face; it's something we cannot see.*

SALTER

My god.

> *Sleeping PETER lowers the hammer to his side. His breathing is still deep. SALTER takes the hammer from him.*

Lighting change: instant transition to a new daytime scene.

PETER quickly exits. SALTER remains beneath the wooden beam, holding onto the hammer. GEORGE enters, sweeping up the evening's debris.

SALTER

(*distracted*) Thank you, Dad.

GEORGE

Now we're a goddamn mess, too.

JENNIFER enters. Pieces of onionskin paper are rolled, like scrolls, in her grip.

JENNIFER

Peter wants you to know he's frightened of himself; he wants to pay for the damages.

SALTER waves this away, on her own mission now. She uses the claw hammer to clear out more space, above the jamb.

SALTER

You brought some of your onionskin paper?

JENNIFER gives SALTER a piece of rubbing charcoal, and a sheet of blank onionskin.

JENNIFER

I did. And I did our side, too, like you asked ...

SALTER is up on her tiptoes now, performing a relief rubbing that we cannot see.

JENNIFER

(*nervous talk*) It's amazing how you don't see something, until you do. (*puzzled*) Our side's been exposed for weeks … I mean, I've looked up there.

SALTER

I have, too, but I didn't make the connection.

GEORGE

(*muttering*) Old wounds …

>   *SALTER finishes with her charcoal rubbing, and makes a request to see JENNIFER's.*

SALTER

Can you show me …?

>   *JENNIFER unrolls the onionskin paper in her own hands. It shows the charcoal rubbing of a "V."*

>   *SALTER nods. Then she places her own, newly completed paper to the left of JENNIFER's. SALTER's paper shows a charcoal rubbing of a "VI."*

JENNIFER

It was never your name at all …

SALTER

It was a six. And a five.

*Lighting change: spotlight at down stage centre. SALTER
steps forward.*

*Behind SALTER, in half-light, GEORGE exits, and JENNIFER
sticks these onionskin papers on the fridge door in the Craigs'
kitchen: "VIV."*

SALTER

Something beneath Peter's waking self had been compelling
him, it seemed. He had revealed one pitch-pine timber, shot like
an arrow through the heart of the house. Older and thicker than
those lesser beams and joists around it, this timber was carved
at either end with a carpenter's mark: in this case, the roman
numerals "Vee-Eye" and "Vee," connecting the beam to the grid
lines six and five on either side of our home's construction.

Roman numerals. Made by Johnson Morris, most likely, back
when he first built the place.

*Behind SALTER, in half-light, JENNIFER and PETER work
inward from either side, completing the "reveal" of this
primary timber.*

*SALTER stands at downstage centre, with the middle of the main
beam behind her and above her. At the middle of the main beam,
JENNIFER and PETER each perform one final charcoal rubbing.*

SALTER

But when the beam was revealed in full, there were six more
numbers waiting to be found. These were straddled on either
side of the wall dividing the main house from the in-law suite.
Our sleepwalker was looking for three numbers in his own
home, and then for three in ours.

But these weren't roman numerals. These weren't
carpenter's marks.

46

These six numbers were made by somebody else entirely: incised in careful digits of a completely different origin.

To one side of SALTER, JENNIFER holds up the charcoal impression of numbers 3, 3, 0. To the other side of SALTER, PETER holds up the impression of numbers 1, 3, 1.

SALTER

Three-three-zero. One-three-one. *(beat)* Put together, they were an official number of registry.

Sound cue: The disembodied booming begins again, lowly, but this time there's a more "hollow" quality to the sound ...

SALTER

We had never known those numbers were up there. Until the Craigs started to renovate, and something from the past awoke, perhaps ... with a wish to be more fully discovered.

In all likelihood, Johnson Morris had found that pitch-pine beam, when it washed up on his beach. And maybe the Craigs weren't living in a haunted house, like they feared ... so much as they were living in a haunted ship.

Sound cue: The booming becomes more recognizable as the hollow of a boat's hull, as it's bashed from without by relentless waves.

Blackout.

End of Act One.

ACT TWO

During the intermission, one final piece of buried architecture has been revealed upon the set. At the back of the implied wall between the Craigs' kitchen and the in-law suite, a vertical post has also been renovated. This vertical post is rounded, with a slight taper: it is a segment of a schooner's mast.

The kitchen set still has plastic sheeting draped at an angle, to cover the counter and the open cabinets. The trap door is again locked with its bicycle chain lock.

From out of the dark, Sister Vivian SALTER emerges in her civilian garb. She begins in direct address –

SALTER

"Mystery" is an interesting word. It belongs to the entire genre my father hates, of course. Other than labelling a detective story, though, its most basic meaning is "something that's difficult or impossible to understand." As in, "what's happening to the couple next door ... remains a mystery to me." But, during the medieval period, "mystery" also blended with the word "mastery," producing a second meaning. Here, "mystery" referred to "the practices, skills, or lore needed to master a particular job." As in, "Can you teach me the tools of your trade? I don't know the mysteries of blacksmithing" ...

And this is where things bend toward religion again. Because during this medieval period, the trade guilds would combine the mysteries of their trades with the mysteries of their faith. Created by the guilds, medieval Mystery Plays celebrated the stories of the Bible as pure entertainment. I wrote about these Mystery Plays, with great enthusiasm, for my dissertation.

This was the popular theatre of its day: thrills, chills, high comedy and low, characters talking directly to the audience ...

SALTER acknowledges her audience –

SALTER
  ... Hi.

The Mystery Plays were filled with stage tricks, special effects and sudden shocks, but all in an attempt to woo people toward God. Each story was presented by the guild who would know its details best: the Goldsmiths would re-enact bringing the "gold, frankincense, and myrrh," for instance, or the Bakers would perform "the Loaves and the Fishes" ...

Lighting change: lights up in the Craigs' kitchen, where GEORGE is seated, sorting coins into pre-rolled tubes. His Memory Box is beside him, labelled as such. JENNIFER is seated with GEORGE, also rolling coins. She wears a scarf over a scoop-neck top. Also on the table is a stack of research papers and books. SALTER switches directly from her audience address into mid-conversation with JENNIFER –

SALTER
  ... or the Shipbuilders would present "Noah and His Ark"! (*beat*) Now, shipbuilders had already been around for thousands of years, of course, but they'd really come into their own, here in Parrsboro, at the time that these numbers were carved –

She points to the main beam, above their heads.

SALTER

Three-three-zero, one-three-one. The official number for *The Torment*, a three-masted schooner built and registered, sailed and wrecked, all around this very harbour.

JENNIFER

If this isn't supernatural, then how could Peter have known the beam was inside the house? You even said he said "torment"!

SALTER

(*brandishing a book*) It's something I'm investigating.

GEORGE keeps arranging coins, with JENNIFER, on the tabletop.

SALTER

And what are you doing, Dad? Counting the family fortune?

GEORGE

I'm finding wrong ones.

JENNIFER

There's never a "wrong one," George. You just put it in a different pile.

GEORGE

Quarters, dimes, nickels; I'm on a roll.

SALTER and JENNIFER are pleasantly surprised.

JENNIFER

Was that a pun, George?

SALTER

I think that was a pun!

GEORGE chuckles to himself. He keeps inspecting, sorting, and rolling.

JENNIFER

(*contemplative*) Doing our sums. (*beat*) Going "back to school" means ... going back to logic. I can't have a ghost story hanging over my head, Vivian, when I teach in September. I have to have it stop.

JENNIFER unwinds her scarf to display the black-and-blue marks over her breastbone.

SALTER

... New bruises ...?

JENNIFER

Don't blame him. Please.

SALTER

He came at me with a claw hammer, dear.

JENNIFER

That wasn't Peter, that night. Not really. (*beat*) And last night, he didn't try to drown himself in the sink ... I did.

SALTER

Oh, no, Jennifer ...

JENNIFER

I was driving myself against the edge of the counter, like I'd break my own ribs. It's what woke me up. (*beat*) But pretty soon, he and me ... we're going to crack.

GEORGE

I won't let anything hurt you.

JENNIFER

(*putting her hand on his*) Thank you, George. (*to SALTER*) As a
teacher, I appreciate the research you've done. I really do.
I appreciate knowing that the main beam is the widest part of
the ship. And that it's where the registration numbers always
got carved, just below deck. I appreciate knowing that the beam
would cross with the mainmast, where that mast ran up from the
keel. (*pointing it out*) That mast. (*beat*) You see, I'm really trying
to listen, and to … understand.

> *JENNIFER leaves the table, fretful. She moves upstage, toward*
> *the newly exposed mast.*

JENNIFER

But I *don't* understand how they could be *right here*: a piece of
that beam, and a piece of that mast …

SALTER

In a lot of cases, shipwrecked timbers got added to barns
or buildings.

JENNIFER

But how could they be calling my husband to unbury them??
(*beat*) Could you read me the record again?

SALTER

(*from a marked page in one book*) Vessel 330-131. Rigging: Tern
Schooner. Gross tonnage: 194. Captain: Geary Spicer. Built in
Parrsboro Harbour, 1900. Came to grief against Black Rock,
inside ten miles of that same harbour, August 27, 1915. Vessel
lost; no souls recovered.

JENNIFER

"No souls …" (*beat*) August 27th is next Sunday.

SALTER

Your point being?

JENNIFER

If everything up to this point has been the "forerunner," then ...
we're not ready for what's coming next. (*beat*) When you offered
me your help, was it as a detective ... or as a nun?

SALTER

What is it you think a nun could accomplish here?

JENNIFER

Contact, maybe? I don't know.

SALTER

Remember, please, my convictions are at ... low ebb.

JENNIFER

Then how can I help you? Maybe we can do it together. Maybe
we can take ... summer's last leap of faith?

Lighting change: spotlight on SALTER as she steps forward.
JENNIFER exits. GEORGE stays behind in the half-light, placing
the rolls of coins into his Memory Box.

SALTER

As Sunday approached, I did more homework. The Age of
Sail Heritage Centre, the Maritime Museum of the Atlantic,
the Canadian Register of Vessels. I combed through logbooks,
manifests, and then more ... pagan texts.

When finished, I told myself this wasn't a "leap of faith,"
so much as a "toe across the line" of what I could believe.
If Jennifer wanted to call the evening a "séance," then so be it.

I'd call it "hypnosis," and use it as best I could. It was for just one night, and I'd known sessions like these to have positive effects, even if they were just placebos.

But perhaps, perhaps, if we could remember the past, then we could all get free of it.

And I'd take a few precautions first.

> *Lighting change: GEORGE is carrying his Memory Box away from the table, but feels that SALTER is in his way –*

GEORGE

Heads up!

SALTER

Wait, that counts for you too, mister. Let me get at your shoulders.

> *SALTER undoes the top buttons of GEORGE's shirt, then wrestles it partway down his back. Once again, she removes GEORGE's old Exelon medical patch ...*

SALTER

Jennifer is going to stay with you later tonight, okay?

GEORGE

Dandy-o.

> *SALTER sticks a new patch onto GEORGE's shoulder blade.*

SALTER

The forecast is for thunder and lightning. I know you hate storms.

GEORGE

(*considers*) No ... (*beat*) It's Viv who hates storms.

SALTER

Well, there you go. You caught me out on something! Because
I'm Viv, right? I'm your daughter.

GEORGE

Then ... who am I?

> *GEORGE and SALTER consider each other for a beat. Then
> SALTER continues in direct address, and GEORGE finishes
> buttoning his clothes.*

SALTER

Um. A deeper conversation than I was expecting to have. But we
did have it, until Jennifer arrived.

> *JENNIFER enters.*

JENNIFER

You ready, George? We're going to have a sleepover!

SALTER

I think he is ready. More ready than I am.

JENNIFER

Hey. When I met you, your aura was dirty grey-silver, guarded
and skeptical. Right now, you're bright.

> *JENNIFER puts her azurite crystal pendant around SALTER's
> neck. SALTER is almost bashful.*

SALTER

Well, this whole thing's a bit of a Hail Mary pass, isn't it?
(*checking in with her*) Precautions?

JENNIFER

(*affirming*) Precautions.

❖   ❖   ❖

Lighting change: While JENNIFER and GEORGE exit right, in the direction of the in-law suite, SALTER dovetails into a new scene with PETER. PETER looks ragged, exhausted.

PETER is pivoted upstage, so we can't see his eyes. His sleeves are rolled up and his tattoos visible. His upstage wrist has a length of rope tied to it. As SALTER begins the scene, she picks up the other end of the rope and ties it to the upstage leg of the kitchen table.

PETER

You don't think this is too many precautions?

SALTER

Claw hammer.

PETER

Okay, okay. *(uncomfortable)* That's pretty tight, Sister: you trying for your merit badge?

SALTER

You've got nuns mixed up with girl scouts, I think. *(beat)* Another detail about those Mystery Plays: What a medieval audience found entertaining wasn't necessarily to our taste. Noah was presented as a very pious man, for instance, very concerned about obeying God's laws. But then, for comic relief, from time to time, like in a Punch and Judy show, Noah would just … beat up on his wife.

SALTER finalizes the knots to keep PETER in place. Each considers the other.

57

PETER

You've read me wrong. (*beat*) I don't want to hurt anybody. And I'd sooner hurt myself than hurt Jennifer. I'm crazy about her.

SALTER

Ain't love grand.

PETER

Hey, you don't want to be here on a Sunday night – neither do I – but I'm the one getting tied to the table.

SALTER

Oh, don't be a crybaby. The last time I was tied to a table, I was holding a live grenade with the pin pulled.

PETER

(*beat*) Really? (*considering*) That's … pretty badass.

SALTER

Yeah. I got my merit badge for it.

They consider each other again, silent, as SALTER puts a storm candle on the table.

PETER

This is craziness, but I'm doing it for her. (*beat*) Why are you?

SALTER lights the candle, then moves around the kitchen to dim all the practical lights. In the gloom, she remains upstage, with PETER's focus on her.

SALTER

When's the last time you slept?

PETER

Without nightmares walking me around …?

He shrugs. SALTER *removes the crystal pendant from
around her neck.*

SALTER

I'm going to get you to look into the candle … and then
we'll begin.

> *Still standing, she places the pendant in front of the candle's
> flame, and then begins to gives the pendant a slow-tempo swing.
> Her tone becomes more soothing.*

PETER

(*recognizing it*) She gave you azurite. She believes it …
transmutes fear.

SALTER

That's good, then. Watch the pulse it creates in the candle. Ten.
(*beat*) Just … give in to the sleep you've been so eager to find.
And know that this can only put you into a state if you want it
to. But for that to happen … maybe we need to trust one another
a little bit better. Nine.

> *Through this countdown,* PETER's *head will incrementally drop.
> His unseen eyes will close.*

PETER

Trust … Okay … Alright …

SALTER

Shhhh.

PETER

(*eventually*) I knew the price of the house was due to
circumstances with your father, but … I still lowballed you. (*beat*)
I'm sorry, it's the nature of my … (*beat*) Nah, you know what …?

I can be a jackass. (*beat*) Jennifer shows me I can be better. (*beat*)
I apologize. Vivian.

SALTER

(*still soothing*) Thank you. Eight. (*volunteering back*) The movie
my father took me to, after he pulled my tooth ...? It was *The
Sound of Music*. Maybe I read you wrong ... and maybe you read
me right. Seven.

> *SALTER keeps hypnotizing PETER, but she speaks in direct
> address. While she speaks, she pivots and sits directly opposite
> her subject, and the angle of PETER's head pivots to follow
> her voice. PETER's closed eyes now become more visible to
> the audience.*

> *In the dark, SALTER's pendant continues to swing in front
> of the candle.*

SALTER

And in the quiet of the night I could hear the small sounds that
an old house makes ... like the cracking of an ancient knuckle.
And it was while counting between the numbers of six ... and
five ... like the six and five embedded in the beam above our
heads ... that Peter fell into a troubled sleep.

> *(Note: The play's pace, from SALTER's hypnosis on until the end,
> should slow down, gathering deliberate power, like a campfire
> ghost story, or a conjuring.)*

SALTER

But then, when I reached four, it was as Jennifer had described,
and the atmosphere around me ... grew charged. And outside,
the rain began to mutter and fall –

> *Sound: rain, gentle at first, which will gain in intensity until
> the play's end.*

SALTER

– but I told myself there was nothing to fear. Three.

There's a strobe of lightning, outside the kitchen's windows. SALTER startles as three very loud cracks of thunder shake the set: BOOM ...! BOOM-BOOM!!

SALTER

Did I mention I hate storms ...? *(beat)* Two.

This time, two booms of thunder come. But accompanying them, PETER, unconscious, also booms his free fist onto the tabletop: BOOM! BOOM!

PETER's fist seems independent of the rest of his body. His head stays slumped. There's a moment's anticipation, while SALTER keeps her pendulum going ...

... When SALTER says "One," there is no exterior thunder, but PETER pounds his fist one single time. His head pops up and his eyes snap open –

SALTER

One.

PETER has no pupils. His eyes have been overtaken, milky white.

61

*(Note: PETER's white contact lenses were inserted before his
Second-Act entrance, but hidden by upstage blocking, selective
low light, and the actor's sleepy eyes.)*

SALTER

(*to herself; committing*) In for a penny, in for a pound. (*beat*)
If you can understand me, can you rap your fist one single time,
to indicate "yes"?

PETER

(THUMP.)

SALTER

Very good, then. (*beat*) And am I communicating, right now,
with Peter Craig?

This time, PETER's fist pounds down twice.

PETER

(*THUMP ... THUMP ...*)

SALTER

I'll take it that two knocks means "No, I'm not." (*beat*) Then
who are you?

PETER

...

SALTER

(*flustered*) Oh, right, you can't answer that one. This occultism is
something of a ... novel experience for me. (*pushing together her
books and research*) Before we begin, I do need to know if Peter is
safe right now.

PETER

(THUMP. THUMP.)

62

SALTER

He's not. Is that because ... something is getting more
powerful in here?

PETER

(THUMP!)

SALTER

Yes. More powerful because we exposed the beam and mast of
The Torment?

PETER

(THUMP ...!)

*SALTER glances into the books before her, her hand splaying
their pages open.*

SALTER

Yes. And this is the night she sank, according to the records.
With no souls recovered. Does that mean ... there were no
souls aboard?

PETER

(THUMP ... THUMP!!)

Outside the windows: a thunderclap and lightning flash.

*At the same time, this stage magic occurs: every dish in the
exposed cabinets shifts laterally to the right. We see what
Jennifer had described in Act One. The kitchen table also shifts
laterally to the right, shoving SALTER back on her heels. SALTER
takes a moment to regather herself, then continues –*

SALTER

Incredible. *(beat)* Are you a member of the crew of *The Torment*?

PETER

(*THUMP.*)

SALTER

(*picking up one of her papers*) Um. I'm Sister Vivian Salter, and
I've brought some manifests. "From Parrsboro to the West
Indies with a cargo of lumber. Return sail in ballast. Crew of
seven." If you're listed among these seven, then ... we can be
properly introduced. (*reading*) Captain Geary Spicer. (*nothing ...*)
First Mate James Merriam. (*nothing ...*) Second Mate Daniel
Smith. (*nothing ...*) Able Seaman Timothy Hicks. (*nothing ...*) Able
Seaman Sam Teed –

PETER

(*THUMP!*)

SALTER

Hello, Sam Teed ... (*beat*) Did you drown aboard *The Torment*?

PETER

...

SALTER

Does that mean you don't know? (*beat; making a connection*)
Wait, I know your name, though –

> *Enthusiastic, she hunts down another piece of paper, this one a
> reproduction of an old newspaper article.*

SALTER

This was in the *Amherst News and Sentinel*, 1915. One
Mr. Samuel Teed, who sailed an entire schooner to Saint John
and back, all by his lonesome, on a coastal run: "three-masted;
single-handed." Was that you ...?

PETER

   (THUMP.)

SALTER

Yes. I understand it was incredibly reckless, and incredibly skilled. A feat of sailing that would make you a local legend … and keep you from crewing ever again. With something to prove, you stole your Captain's ship, however briefly.

PETER

   …

SALTER

It took me a while to find that article, actually, because the ship wasn't called *The Torment* anymore. *(beat)* When I read through the Shipping Registers a second time, I noted that Sailing Vessel 330-131 had been rechristened, in 1913.

PETER

   …

SALTER

A happier name, the *Maggie Ann*. Markedly less torment. *(beat)* But isn't it bad luck, for a ship to change her name?

PETER

   (THUMP.)

SALTER

And yet Captain Geary Spicer did it anyway. *(bringing another paper close)* Marriages are also a matter of public record. I can guess that Captain Spicer changed his schooner's name, in order to honour his brand-new bride …? Maggie Ann Spicer, almost forty years his junior?

The wind outside is beginning to pick up force, as is the lashing of the rain.

SALTER

Spicer was enamoured. A graying old salt, with a reason at last to retire. And to retire his vessel as well. (*beat*) By 1915, even with a new name, the schooner's best years would've been behind her.

PETER

(*angrily: THUMP! THUMP!*)

SALTER

No?

Another flash of lightning, and crack of thunder. This time, it results in the power going out: what moody practical lighting there was is now reduced to nil.

SALTER

Aw, the power ...

SALTER stands in the dark, spooked, and PETER remains sitting.

SALTER

Mr. Teed, if you'll let Peter know that I'm borrowing his flashlight ...?

SALTER rummages in the cupboard below the sink until she finds a six-volt flashlight. She turns it on, and it becomes nearly the entire illumination for the scene. When SALTER points her light into PETER's face, his supernatural white eyes are disturbing.

SALTER

Now where were we …? (*beat*) You'd been with Captain
Spicer for more years than his own mates … but he never let
you rise. For all your talent, you'd been denied your Master's
Certificate. Why?

> *Unable to answer yes or no to this question,* PETER *instead
> grabs the reproduction article from the* Amherst News *and*
> Sentinel. *He shoves it at* SALTER *again, tapping his finger at
> its final paragraph.*

SALTER

"Using only the lower sails, Mr. Teed followed along the tides,
safely drifting the *Maggie Ann* into Parrsboro Harbour: three-
masted; single-handed. Stepping ashore to much wonderment,
and to many questions, Mr. Teed could only answer them all
with a doffing of his cap, and, as ever, a silent nod." (*absorbing
this* …) As ever, a silent nod. (*looking at him*) Mr. Teed, forgive
me. This is my first time establishing "paranormal rapport" …
In life, were you also unable to speak?

PETER

  (… *THUMP.*)

SALTER

I see. (*beat*) You wanted to captain the *Maggie Ann* yourself, but
disability kept you from her.

JENNIFER

Not quite.

SALTER and PETER startle, shoving back their chairs, though PETER is still tied to the table. SALTER trains her flashlight toward the left doorway, illuminating JENNIFER, her pale figure half-obscured. JENNIFER is wearing a long dress from the turn of the nineteenth century. She is soaked to the bone; her eyes are also a pupilless white.

JENNIFER

You chose the wrong "her."

JENNIFER's voice is eerie. While she speaks, she takes very slow, sloshing steps toward PETER. She holds her hands together prettily, as her dress drips behind her.

SALTER

Maggie Ann Spicer?

JENNIFER

I can speak for him. Sam has been tongue-tied since birth. Mute. He could hear orders, but not convey them; and when my husband decided his schooner was no longer fit for the sea, he was forcing that decision upon Sam, as well. (*beat*) But Sam was strong, physical, proud. When he sailed into port that day, all alone, he did it to prove that he could. And, after that, everyone knew that both the man and the vessel shouldn't be discounted. (*beat*) And I knew that I loved him. Salt water on his skin, every bead of it still holding warmth from the August sun.

SALTER

This is August. This is the night of the twenty-seventh. Is this why you're here?

The sounds of the storm begin to slowly transform. They hollow out, like they're being heard from inside the hull of a rocking, wooden ship.

JENNIFER

When a boat sinks, it creates an undertow, dragging us back ...

SALTER

Are you saying you were aboard *The Torment* that night – ?
(*correcting herself*) The *Maggie Ann*?

JENNIFER

Do you know what charivari is?

SALTER

Um, a sometimes tradition in a small town, I believe. To show
disapproval for an "unnatural" wedding.

JENNIFER

Like the wedding of a man in wither, and a girl in bloom. A poor
girl of no means, ill-promised, and with no say. The hecklers,
they bang their pots and pans at you, they jeer and din on your
wedding night, and they call it "rough music." Do you know
how terrible it is to become a bride that way?

SALTER

I don't.

JENNIFER

But in the middle of all that noise, and in every way opposite
to it, was Sam. The best listener I had ever known ... And for
the next two years, he listened as I described the "rough music"
my husband – pious and cruel – made with his fists upon me.

PETER

(*THUMP!*)

JENNIFER

We plotted our escape. If Sam could sail the *Maggie Ann* once,
all by himself ... then we would do it again, together. (*beat*)

We made it to the ship under cover of darkness; we hadn't breathed our plans to a soul. (*beat*) But then we were undone by the August Gales, tangling us in sudden weather.

> *Stage magic: The kitchen table magically shoves to the left. At the same time, the lamp hanging above the table also swings to the left, of its own accord. The contents of the cupboards also shift left, beyond the construction plastic ...*
>
> *... And then all these objects shift to the right. From side to side, this "rocking" sequence repeats. The actors mimic these effects, as well, putting a small, uneasy sway into their knees.*

SALTER

(*direct address*) Seasick unreality pitches the room, and me in it.

JENNIFER

For a hundred years, Sam's been hunting for what happened next: he doesn't remember. (*beat*) Despite our escape ... the Captain was waiting for us on board. He attacked from behind, smashing Sam's head against the main mast, like a bottle of champagne. (*touching PETER's head*) All the strength went out of Sam's body, and out of my will. Trapped, alone, my husband forced me to confess to our lovers' sins. And when I did, he abandoned us both here. (*beat*) Sam, without me, might have been able to overcome the gale. But me, without him, well ... I am no sailor, and I could not. (*beat*) We came to grief, in every way, against Black Rock; we drowned between six o'clock and five o'clock on that red morning.

SALTER

Drowned. (*beat*) And when the mast and the beam washed to shore, some time later, innocent Johnson Morris was simply there to repurpose them. Into the construction of this house.

*JENNIFER holds out her hands to SALTER, in a
supplicating gesture.*

JENNIFER

We're trapped here by our sins. But shouldn't the sin of infidelity
be forgiven by the truth of love…? You're a woman of faith, and
I believe you can set us free.

SALTER

I … don't know how.

*JENNIFER pats down her own wet body, her own wet face, to
indicate that it is a foreign "vessel" to her –*

JENNIFER

If we can't get free, then these vessels will also drown. Jennifer
and Peter will drown. These vessels that are your friends. (*beat*)
But not if you can save our souls.

All of the sounds and stage magic are building to a crescendo.

SALTER

(*earnest*) During my mission, I've … punished some people, I've
put them into prison, but I don't know that I've ever really, truly,
saved a soul. (*less earnest*) Unfortunately, I don't think I'm going
to start with you guys.

JENNIFER

(*beat*) What?

71

SALTER

These last few months, I've been lost, wondering if I am too cynical for sentiments like "true love." So ... it's nice to be reminded that cynicism can serve a purpose too. You see, just because you're communing with the dead, doesn't mean the dead aren't trying to bullshit you.

JENNIFER

(*puzzled*) Why ... why would you blaspheme?

SALTER

Oh, you're in the twenty-first century now, sister. (*beat*) You described the Captain as "a man in wither," then tried to tell me he knocked out your "strong, physical" Sam. So did he dodder, or did he domineer ...? (*beat*) Might there be a version of events where Sam got the upper hand – two against one, after all – and then you threw the weak, old man into his own hold? Locking him down there?

> *An insistent hammering begins against the underside of the trap door. Still chain-locked, the trap door only pops up an inch every time. Fog spills upward from inside the trap, accompanied by a supernatural light.*

SALTER

You described yourself as a "poor girl," with no say, and no means. Might that girl not see the value in her married Captain going down with his own ship? And during a convenient August Gale? Ships are highly insured, after all; shipwrecks are terribly plentiful; and wives are direct beneficiaries. (*beat*) If you concede that this might be so, then wouldn't it also be shrewd to make your accomplice a man who literally can't talk?

> *PETER yanks against his restraints, with growing aggression or desperation. The sound makes a "rough music" in concert with the hammering of the hatch.*

JENNIFER

You can't help us this way; you can help us by freeing us –

SALTER moves her flashlight from JENNIFER to PETER, then back again, while telling this second version of events.

SALTER

But what if your accomplice was surprised, when you made your mercenary suggestion? What if Sam was unwilling to murder the master and commander who gave him opportunity, just for the sake of your conjugal bed? (*beat*) Maybe that's when the two of *you* ended up fighting, and then you shoved Sam, at the exact moment that the decks pitched and rolled – smashing Sam, by accident, into that main mast. And maybe this entire altercation was heard, by the frail Captain trapped below. Maybe he heard you panic, in your folly and your greed, as you realized that neither mariner was with you now: unmoored, and with that Black Rock growing bigger and bigger, just off your bow.

The construction plastic snaps out to one side, catching a full, supernatural wind. The plastic now resembles a schooner's sail.

JENNIFER

You can believe what you want to believe.

SALTER

But here's the thing: you said you had no idea how the Captain knew how to find you on board; that you hadn't breathed your plans to a soul.

SALTER slides an old paper out of one of her books. She holds it aloft.

73

SALTER

Then why did you leave him this letter? Begging him not
to follow you ... but then clearly indicating at what time
and what place?

JENNIFER

(*rattled*) Where did you ...?

SALTER

... Find it? (*beat*) It's certainly a letter that reads like
incriminating bait. The kind that a canny wife would surely
destroy, if she had lived to return to land.

> *PETER looks at JENNIFER, sensing betrayal. JENNIFER looks at
> SALTER with black hate.*

JENNIFER

... Every nunnery hides a whore.

> *There's another peal of thunder and lightning.*

SALTER

Why don't you step out of that nice couple, and say
that to my face.

> *Seemingly from nowhere, JENNIFER produces the lost Vise-Grips
> and raises them high above her head, like a knife. A terror
> tableau. She shrieks and charges across the stage, on the attack.*
>
> *Stage magic: When JENNIFER shrieks, all the kitchen drawers
> pop open, the cutlery within them clattering.*
>
> *As abruptly as her attack begins, JENNIFER now crumples to the
> ground, losing all consciousness.*
>
> *While the sound design and stage magic mostly ebb to nothing,
> SALTER moves to check on JENNIFER.*

SALTER kneels beside JENNIFER, and peels two objects from her neighbour's wet shoulder blade. Up to this point, these objects were hidden from sight under JENNIFER's antique dress.

SALTER holds the objects up, waving them in PETER's general direction. They're a double dose of George's medical patches, and they've had their cumulative side effect: JENNIFER has fainted.

SALTER

Precautions. (*beat*) Jennifer's own idea. "Multiple patches eventually produce fainting."

SALTER gives the unconscious woman an affectionate pat. She then stands and asks the still-bound spectre –

SALTER

Mr. Teed, did you know that I was bluffing about Maggie Ann's letter?

PETER

(*after a moment: Thump. Thump.*)

SALTER

I didn't have it. (*beat*) Though, up to a certain point, she did have me: certainly I can empathize with a young woman who felt trapped, and desperate to change her life's course. But not when plotting that course meant ending the lives of others.

I'd heard about her premeditated letter, you see, in the conversation I had with Captain Spicer, earlier this evening –

SALTER moves to the trap door and opens it. Supernatural light still arcs from the hatch, in its dissipating fog.

SALTER

He'd been wondering who he was, and, well ... I trusted him on sight.

SALTER extends her hand and helps GEORGE to exit the trap.
GEORGE's outfit splits the difference between antique and
modern day. He is not soaked. He is not wearing white contact
lenses.

SALTER

Maybe because I liked the look of his face. This third ghost, you
see, who'd been sharing a vessel, for how long I don't know, with
my father's own foggy mind.

SALTER

The theory we were testing tonight was that "remembering the
past, we might be able to get free of it." But trapped Captain
Spicer tells me that, for mariners, there is one more step. A mast-
step, to be precise. (*beat*) It wasn't a ceremony I knew anything
about. A coin placed between the mast and the mast-step, for
luck … but also to pay the ferryman if you drowned at sea, and
you needed to cross into the afterlife. And should that coin
become lost on a wounded, sinking ship, well …

GEORGE hands a silver coin to SALTER, passing it to her across
the light of the trap. The coin shines.

SALTER

… it is all a matter of what you believe. (*to GEORGE*) You
finally found the right one, Captain? After all your wounds,
and searching?

GEORGE

(*eerie*) 1900. The year that she was launched.

SALTER turns the coin to tails, confirming this date. She moves
upstage toward the mast. GEORGE makes a small correction –

76

GEORGE

(*eerie*) Oh, and Sister ...? Head's up.

*With a small nod, SALTER flips the coin to heads. With her
back to us, SALTER places the coin against the mast. There's
a sense of religious ceremony to this, almost like the coin is a
communion wafer. As the light from the trap door burns whiter
and whiter, it cuts through the horizontal main beam and the
vertical main mast ... making, perhaps, the steep shadow of a
Catholic crucifix.*

*Thunder rumbles one more time, but in the rolling distance now,
letting us know that the storm has passed.*

SALTER

Fare well, seafarer.

*When SALTER turns around, she steps to the trap door and
lowers it. After it closes, the practical stage lights return to
normalcy: the power is back on. SALTER turns off her flashlight.*

She directs her next speech only to GEORGE, who listens to her –

SALTER

And the three drowned spirits were freed, and the ship went
back to sleep ... and the ghost story ended. Do you remember
this story now, Dad?

During this next, PETER and JENNIFER move about the set,
reassembling it. This is like their "construction dumb show"
from Act One. They close all the open drawers. They take the
plastic sheeting down from the cupboards. They remove the
charcoal drawings from the fridge, etc. When they're done, the
kitchen appears ready for new sale.

SALTER

Our night's homework was over, and nothing incredible ever
happened again. Well ... depending on how you define the word.
(*beat*) Jennifer's teaching year began. Peter sold some cars. And
their marriage proved to be ... good. Better than good, in fact.
Maybe I'd even say "true." (*beat*) But they didn't stay here. Not
in this house. After the summer, who could really blame them?

GEORGE

The place was a goddamn mess.

SALTER

(*laughing*) Yes, it was.

PETER and JENNIFER exit together, via the upstage kitchen door
to "outside."

SALTER

I know it's statistically unlikely at my age, Dad, but you'll be
happy to know I kept them both as friends: I finally made a few.
(*beat; taking the plunge*) ... They even came to your funeral.

GEORGE

Oh?

SALTER begins to tidy GEORGE's outfit: primping his collar,
fiddling with his suspenders.

SALTER

You and Jennifer and Peter: you were all haunted in this house, so … why wasn't I? Well. I'm haunted by you. (*beat*) "Remember the past, in order to get free of it" …

SALTER tries not to let her emotions get the better of her, but …

SALTER

When you died, it didn't happen at Mount Hope. It happened here, under your own roof. It was quiet, it was the middle of the afternoon, and I still wasn't ready. (*beat*) I just didn't feel like a lot of good things could possibly come after …

But the world can be good: Jennifer and Peter just had their first kid. Would you believe they call me Sister Godmother now …?

GEORGE

Good, that's good …

SALTER takes GEORGE by the hand.

SALTER

I held your onionskin hand, and your breath stopped, and you weren't scared …

… You didn't know who I was, but it was better than I'd feared.

She begins to lead him from the kitchen area into the in-law suite, and toward that stage-right door in the vestibule –

SALTER

The house is for sale again, Dad. Our Whitehall House. I'll lock it up, one last time, when we're both ready.

When GEORGE steps through the doorway, he stops and puts something in SALTER's hand. It's another silver coin.

SALTER

What's this one …?

GEORGE

1958. The year that she was born. (*really seeing her*) You. Vivian Rose. My girl.

SALTER

(*thankful; quiet*) … Solved.

> *GEORGE turns and walks away. SALTER gives her nonchalant saying a more substantial meaning, this third and final time:*

SALTER

Well. There … you … go.

> *And, indeed, GEORGE is now gone. SALTER turns back into the in-law suite, alone. She shows the coin to us.*

SALTER

In for a penny, in for a pound. Believe.

> *She puts the coin in her pocket. From that same pocket, she discovers her rosary. She takes that rosary out.*

SALTER

Mary's apparition also gave us Glorious Mysteries, like "the grace of a happy death."

SALTER retrieves the tailor's dummy she put to one side; it's dressed in the formal pieces of her nun's habit.

SALTER rolls that tailor's dummy back to centre, and begins to put her habit back on during this final direct address –

Lighting change: spotlight on SALTER.

SALTER

Whether this was quite so much of a Bluenose Gothic, or whether I embellished here and there, I'll leave up to you. But do remember that the Mystery Plays, in their effects, were foremost meant to entertain. They also tried, as I mentioned, to renew a dormant spark of wonder, perhaps, and an engagement with the wholly unknowable. And for this reason, over time, the word "mystery" in those entertainments became interchangeable with the word "miracle." The Miracle Play. (*beat*)

Did we touch upon mystery that summer, my father and I? Certainly. Did we touch upon something more, for a moment, that … brought my father back to me? Well, perhaps. Perhaps. It is something I'm … ready again to contemplate.

Dressed, SALTER puts her rosary back around her neck. She describes its mysteries –

SALTER

This rosary was given to Saint Dominic, and then to us all, for those very same contemplations. Joyful, Sorrowful, and Glorious Mysteries; joined now in the modern era, sometimes, by Luminous.

With her fingers, SALTER counts the beads of her rosary, following its loop toward the end.

SALTER

Each to be considered, in turn, for an entire cycle of five decades. Bringing me, at the last, to a place where I'm able to start again. Where I'm renewed. Because coming around to this, my *next* decade, only means that a new mystery ... is about to begin.

SALTER stands before us, assembled, and ready.

Blackout.

End of play.

ACKNOWLEDGMENTS

I'd like to thank Conrad Byers, Kerwin Davison, Patricia O'Neal, Roger Marsters, and Mark Gillis for all their expertise and strength-testing. I'd like to thank Don Hannah, Jenny Munday, and the Playwrights Atlantic Resource Centre, as well as Arts Nova Scotia and the Playwrights Guild of Canada, for their invaluable support. I'd like to thank director Natasha MacLellan, the cast, crew, and entire design team for reading this script and saying yes: like Viv, they chose to embrace the impossible.

ABOUT THE AUTHOR

Josh MacDonald is the writer of the stage plays *Degrees*, *Halo*, and *Whereverville*. Published by Talonbooks, *Halo* and *Whereverville* are curriculum titles in Nova Scotia high schools. *Halo* has been produced around North America, and been adapted into the feature film *Faith, Fraud & Minimum Wage* (Entertainment One), for which MacDonald wrote the screenplay. MacDonald is also the writer of the horror feature *The Corridor* (IFC Films / D Films) which played around the world and won the "Next Wave" Award for Best Screenplay at Fantastic Fest in Austin, Texas. He is the writer-director of the short film *Game*, viewed more than a million times online. He has written for CBC Television and Radio, the National Film Board of Canada, the Smithsonian Channel, Reelz, Blue Ant Media, and others. Josh has taught creative writing at the Nova Scotia College of Art and Design (NSCAD University) and the Fountain School of Performing Arts at Dalhousie University. Also a professional actor for stage and screen, MacDonald is married to actor Francine Deschepper.